DON'T BE SHY

By Anna H. Dickson • Illustrated by Tom Cooke

With thanks to Marty Robinson, who plays Mr. Snuffle-upagus on *Sesame Street*.
Olivia is performed by Alaina Reed, and David is performed by Northern Calloway.

A SESAME STREET / GOLDEN PRESS BOOK
Published by Western Publishing Company, Inc., in conjunction with Children's Television Workshop.

Olivia asked her friends to stand on the steps of 123 Sesame Street so that she could take a picture of them. Just as she was going to snap the picture, she noticed that someone was missing—Mr. Snuffle-upagus!

"Come and get in the picture, Snuffie!" Olivia called to him. "Don't be shy!"

Big Bird wanted to play double-Dutch jump rope with Betty Lou and Ernie, but he needed a partner. Then he saw Snuffie watching.

"I see you, Mr. Snuffle-upagus!" Big Bird called. "Won't you help me turn the jump ropes?"

"I can't, Bird," Snuffie answered. "I don't know how."

"Come on, Snuffie!" Big Bird said. "We'll teach you. Don't be shy!"

Snuffie and Big Bird turned the ropes together and sang while Ernie and Betty Lou jumped.

"Betty Lou, Betty Lou, turn around!
Ernie, Ernie, touch the ground!"

"See, Snuffie?" said Big Bird. "You're just the right size to help me. Later you can learn to jump rope, too."

When Great-Aunt Snuffle-upagus came to visit, Snuffie was too shy to greet her.

"This is your aunt Agnes," said Snuffie's mommy. "You haven't seen her since you were a little ball of snuffle fur. Say hello to Aunt Agnes, dear."

But Snuffie hid behind his mother.

"What's the matter, Snuffie?" asked Aunt Agnes. "Has the cat got your snuffle?"

When he went to Hooper's Store, Snuffie was too
timid to ask David for what he wanted to buy. Ernie
bought bubble soap and blew colorful bubbles into the
air. Bert bought some stripey shoestrings and laced up
his saddle shoes.

"See you later," they said, and they went home.

Still Snuffie hung back and did not ask David for
anything.

Finally David asked, "Would you like something, Snuffie?"

"Yes, David," Snuffie answered slowly. "Um..."

"What is it, Snuffie?" asked David.

"May I please have a package of baseball cards?"

"Sure, Snuffie," answered David. "Why didn't you say so?"

"I hope I get a Ron Adorable card," drawled Snuffie.

When Snuffie went to Grover's house for lunch, he snuffled down his yummy spaghetti in two minutes flat. It was so delicious that he wished he could have a second helping.

Grover's mother noticed that Snuffie's plate was empty. "Would you like some more spaghetti, Snuffie?" she asked. "And another glass of milk? Don't be shy."

Still Life
with Cabbages

snuffie

Betty Lou

Big Bird

One day the mayor came to Sesame Street. He came
to give the prize for the best painting in the Sesame
Street Art Fair.

"And the winner is...Mr. Snuffle-upagus!" announced
the mayor.

Everybody clapped and cheered. "Where's Snuffie?"
asked Betty Lou. "He won the blue ribbon."

But Snuffie had disappeared. He was too shy to stand
up in front of everyone to accept his prize.

At play group the other kids showed their treasures in show-and-tell. But Snuffie was too shy to show the conch shell Aunt Agnes had brought him from Hawaii.

When Miss Tighe asked if anyone could read the word on the board, Snuffie didn't raise his snuffle, even though he knew what the word said.

STOP

During music everyone sang, "Sunny day, clearing the clouds away." But Snuffie sang so softly that no one could hear his gravelly Snuffle-upagus voice.

At his own surprise birthday party Snuffie was too shy to come out and open his presents. Only when he had to blow out the candles on his birthday cake did Snuffie come out of the kitchen.

"Snuff out all the candles, Snuffie!" said Betty Lou. "Don't be shy!"

On the day of *The Sesame Street Weather Play*, everyone was getting ready for the performance. Ernie as RAIN and Bert as SNOW put on their costumes and practiced their lines. Cookie Monster as WIND breezed around them. But Snuffie felt stage shy.

"Where is the SUN?" asked Prairie Dawn, the director. "Where is Snuffie?"

Prairie Dawn found the Snuffle-sun hiding in the stage curtain.

"Snuffie!" she said. "Please come out. How can we have the play without you? How can we tell our weather story without you?

"The sun must come out! Don't be shy."

"Oh, dear," said Snuffie.

So the play began. The snow fell, and the wind blew, and the rain splashed and splashed until, finally, Mr. Snuffle-upagus took a deep breath and said in his deep snuffle voice, "All right, Prairie. The show must go on."

And so the sun came out!

When the play was over, the audience clapped
and cheered. The actors bowed proudly.
Mr. Snuffle-upagus smiled and waved his snuffle
at the audience.

Then Snuffie saw Prairie Dawn standing behind the
curtain, out of sight. He lumbered over and pulled her
out onto the stage.

"Come and take a bow, Prairie!" he said.
"Don't be shy!"